The
Tiara
Club

For Princess Alice of Orchard,
with lots of love, x
VF

For Alan, Lucy
and Steph
SG

www.tiaraclub.co.uk

ORCHARD BOOKS
338 Euston Road, London NW1 3BH
Orchard Books Australia
Hachette Children's Books
Level 17/207 Kent Street, Sydney, NSW 2000, Australia
A Paperback Original
First published in Great Britain in 2005
Text © copyright Vivian French 2005
Illustrations © copyright Sarah Gibb 2005
The rights of Vivian French and Sarah Gibb to be
identified as the author and illustrator of this work
have been asserted by them in accordance with
the Copyright, Designs and Patents Act, 1988.

A CIP catalogue record for this book is available
from the British Library.
ISBN 1 84362 861 9
5 7 9 10 8 6

Printed in Great Britain

The Tiara Club

Princess Alice
and the Magical Mirror

By Vivian French

Illustrated by Sarah Gibb

ORCHARD BOOKS

The Royal Palace Academy
for the Preparation of Perfect Princesses

(Known to our students as ' The Princess Academy')

OUR SCHOOL MOTTO:
*A Perfect Princess always thinks of others before herself,
and is kind, caring and truthful.*

We offer the complete curriculum for all princesses, including –

*How to talk
to a Dragon*

*Designing and Creating
the Perfect Ball Gown*

*Creative Cooking for
Perfect Palace Parties*

*Avoiding Magical
Mistakes*

*Wishes, and how
to use them Wisely*

*Descending a Staircase
as if Floating on Air*

Our head teacher, Queen Gloriana, is present at all times, and students are well looked after by the school Fairy Godmother.

Visiting tutors and experts include –

*KING PERCIVAL
(Dragons)*

*QUEEN MOTHER MATILDA
(Etiquette, Posture and Poise)*

*LADY VICTORIA
(Banquets)*

*THE GRAND HIGH DUCHESS
DELIA (Costume)*

We award tiara points to encourage
our princesses towards the next level.
All princesses who win enough points in their
first year are welcomed to the Tiara Club
and presented with a silver tiara.

Tiara Club princesses are invited to return
next year to Silver Towers, our very special
residence for Perfect Princesses, where
they may continue their education
at a higher level.

PLEASE NOTE:
Princesses are expected to arrive at the Academy
with a *minimum* of:

TWENTY BALL GOWNS
*(with all necessary hoops,
petticoats, etc)*

TWELVE DAY DRESSES

SEVEN GOWNS
*suitable for garden parties,
and other special
day occasions*

TWELVE TIARAS

DANCING SHOES
five pairs

VELVET SLIPPERS
three pairs

RIDING BOOTS
two pairs

*Cloaks, muffs, stoles, gloves
and other essential
accessories as required*

Hi! I've been LONGING to meet you – you're the BEST!! Not like horrible Princess Perfecta, and Princess Floreen. Sometimes they're SO spiteful! My big sister says it's because Perfecta didn't get NEARLY enough tiara points to join the FANTASTIC Tiara Club last year, so now she's back in the first year with us. Poor us!

I'm Princess Alice, by the way. I'm learning to be a Perfect Princess at the Princess Academy, just like you, but you know what school is like – HARD WORK! If it wasn't for Charlotte, Katie, Emily, Daisy and Sophia, I think I'd COLLAPSE! And I don't know about you, but I just can't be good ALL the time...

Chapter One

Have you ever been to a Garden Party? We have one every term here at the Princess Academy, and they are SUCH fun – at least, that's what my big sis says. She says everyone dresses up in their VERY best dresses and tiaras, and a huge orchestra arrives to play dance music, and the fountains splash sparkling lemonade. There are flowers just EVERYWHERE...and all our relations are invited to come and see just how Perfect we are! And if it looks like rain, guess what happens? Fairy G – that's the school Fairy Godmother – floats a sunny blue sky over the whole garden!! Isn't that just SO amazing?

There's another FANTASTIC thing about the Garden Party. It's the one and only time when Fairy G brings out the Princess Academy Magical Mirror...and it really is MAGICAL! My big sis made me PROMISE I wouldn't tell anyone what happens because it's supposed to be a really HUGE surprise, but I know it's OK to tell you. This (sh! Don't tell ANYONE!) is what happens...

On Garden Party day, every princess in the Princess Academy puts on one of her special dresses, does her hair, and puts on her tiara. Then each princess is invited into Fairy G's private study to curtsey to her reflection.

And GUESS WHAT?

The Magical Mirror looks right back, and decides how much of a Perfect Princess you are – and it gives you tiara points!

And it can give you up to THREE
HUNDRED!!!! But my big sister
says nobody has EVER got that
many.

So you can see why I was
counting every single minute until
Garden Party day – but of course
there was a BAD side to it as well.

Suddenly we had DOZENS of extra classes in *Curtseying to the Floor*, and *Walking Gracefully in Long Skirts*, and *Dancing*...oh, we had to learn HUNDREDS of new dances! It seemed as if we NEVER had even half a second to have any fun.

But we did our best and at last there was only one day to go. Our dresses were already hanging up on the rail in our dormitory.

My dress was SO dreamy – it was totally TOTALLY gorgeous pale pink satin, scattered with the sweetest little pink and white daisies, and it had layers and layers of silk petticoats, so it rustled beautifully as I walked! Our tiaras were sparkling on dark blue velvet cushions on our bedside chairs. We were wildly excited...until everything went SO wrong.

On the Thursday morning we had our final test in *Descending the Staircase as if Floating on Air* – and all six of us failed miserably, especially me.

Queen Mother
Matilda (she's the
school Visiting Expert
in Etiquette, Posture, Poise
and Deportment) got REALLY
cross, and ordered us to practice
every spare moment we had.

"If you don't improve DRAMATICALLY by tomorrow evening," she snapped, "you will spend the day of the Garden Party in your dormitory!" And then she glared at us, and swept away.

We did as we were told, but we didn't seem to get any better. By Friday tea time I was SO worried. What if Queen Mum Mattie said we couldn't go to the Garden Party? That would be TOTALLY TERRIBLE...because we'd never get to see the Magical Mirror and win our tiara points!!

"My feet hurt!" Charlotte moaned as we dragged ourselves up the Grand Staircase for what felt like the hundredth time since breakfast.

"Maybe we'll just SAIL down this time," Katie said hopefully.

"NO chance," I said gloomily.

"I fell over about ten times this morning."

"Head UP, breathe IN, STRAIGHTEN your back, and SMILE!" Emily and Daisy chanted together.

"And DON'T forget to curtsey on the second to bottom step!" Sophia added as we reached the top landing.

We all groaned loudly.

"Ooooh! Floreen, DO look!" Horrid Princess Perfecta suddenly appeared with her nasty friend.

"It's the dozy rosie-posies!"

Floreen gave us a pitying smile. "So it is! Isn't it a shame that they're only Perfect Princesses when it comes to FALLING down stairs!" And she and Perfecta sniggered loudly as they went off along the corridor.

I pretended I hadn't heard them, and stared out of the window. Outside in the sunny garden the three kitchen maids, Moira, Prue and Jinny, were running to and fro with armfuls of flowers. Usually they're kept busy inside by the Academy cook, Big Clara, but today they were arranging HUGE vases of lilies and roses and big white daisies all the way down the drive and around the courtyard of the Princess Academy.

"Aren't they LUCKY?" I said to Emily. "They don't have to worry about how to walk down a stupid staircase!"

"I suppose." Emily looked doubtful. "But just IMAGINE having Big Clara ordering you about every second of the day!"

Emily was right about Big Clara being bossy. Prue had obviously put one of the vases in the wrong place in the courtyard, because Big Clara was jumping about in a rage, and shouting at her. I could see Prue was trying not to cry as she picked up the vase, and it must have been REALLY heavy because she went bright red as she struggled with it. And then she just happened to look up at the window, and she saw me looking, and she tried SO hard to smile at me...and I felt so sorry for her I made a funny face, and pretended to jump about just like Big Clara.

BIG MISTAKE!

Prue laughed...

...and she DROPPED the vase...

...and it SMASHED into a thousand pieces and SQUASHED all the flowers!

And at exactly that moment I heard a stern voice from the corridor below calling, "Princesses! Let me see you FLOAT down that staircase!"

Chapter Two

I didn't know WHAT to do! It was COMPLETELY my fault that Prue had dropped the flowers. I SO wanted to rush out to the garden...but Queen Mum Mattie was standing at the bottom of the staircase with a grim look on her face.

I made up my mind.

I would FLOAT down the staircase, and then DASH outside and explain to Big Clara.

"Listen!" I whispered urgently as I pushed in front of Charlotte. "I've got to go first...I've done something AWFUL!"

Then I took a deep breath.

"Head UP, back STRAIGHT, SMILE!" I said to myself...and I tripped on the first step...and rolled ALL the way down...and fell RIGHT in front of Queen Mother Matilda in a heap.

"GRACIOUS, Princess Alice," she said. "Are you all right?"

"Yes, thank you," I said.

"Erm— EXCUSE ME!" and I shot off down the marble corridor and out through the garden door.

I found Moira and Jinny crying on the steps in a muddle of broken china and crushed flowers.

"Where's Big – I mean, where's Cook?" I gasped.

Moira sniffed loudly. "She's FURIOUS, Princess Alice. She's gone into the kitchen and she's locked the door. And she's sent Prue to polish ALL the silver in the scullery, and if we don't clear up this mess and find new flowers by six o'clock we won't be allowed to go to the Garden Party. We'll have to spend ALL DAY peeling potatoes instead!"

I felt even worse. I was almost certain I wouldn't be going to the Garden Party myself – but this was DREADFUL. I began to pick up some of the flower heads, but Moira stopped me.

"You can't do that, Princess Alice," she said. "You'll get into BIG trouble if you're seen! Princesses aren't allowed in the gardens until tomorrow!"

And that was when I had a BRILLIANT idea!

"QUICK!" I said. "Where's the scullery?"

It was really hard to persuade Prue to swap clothes with me, but I did it in the end.

"If I pretend I'm a kitchen maid I can help Jinny and

32

Moira," I explained, "and then I'll swap back with you, and tell Big Clara it was my fault you dropped the vase!"

Prue began to giggle as she picked up yet another fork. "You did look funny," she said. "You looked JUST like Big Clara!

And I'll try not to spoil your dress – promise!"

"And I'll try not to spoil yours!" I said as I followed Moira and Jinny into the garden.

It took us AGES to clean up the mess. The bits of china had scattered everywhere, and we had to find every single piece. Then we had to find more flowers, and Jinny said we weren't meant to take ANY without asking the gardeners.

"Big Clara had a right old row with the Head Gardener as it was," she said.

Moira sighed. "I knew it was no good, even with you trying so hard, Princess Alice. And it's half past five already. We'll be peeling potatoes tomorrow, no mistake."

For a terrible moment I thought Moira was right – and then I had my SECOND brilliant idea!

"I KNOW!" I said. "Why don't we take just one or two flowers from each of the other vases? I don't think it would EVER show…"

So that's what we did. And it didn't take long at all to fill the vase that Jinny had brought out with her from the scullery, and the flowers looked GORGEOUS. You'd never have known there had been an accident at all.

"Time for me and Prue to change back again." I said happily. "I hope she's not too worn out polishing all those knives and forks and spoons!"

But when Moira and Jinny and I burst into the scullery, there was nothing there but a heap of gleaming silver cutlery.

Prue was GONE.

Chapter Three

I stood and stared with my eyes popping out of my head. Moira rushed off one way to see if Prue was in her bedroom, and Jinny dashed the other way to see if she was in the kitchen.

Moira came back almost at once, shaking her head.

"She's not there," she said.

And then there was a HUMUNGOUS roar, and Big Clara was standing in front of us waving a soup ladle. Jinny was behind her, looking pale.

I tried to make myself look as tall and as dignified as possible, although my heart was pounding.

"I am Princess Alice," I began, "and I'm so sorry, but it was my fault that Prue broke the vase—"

"WHAT? WHAT'S THAT? WHAT on EARTH are you talking about?"

I'm sure that the entire Princess Academy must have heard Big Clara shouting. I took a deep breath, and tried again.

"I was looking out of the window, and—"

"PRUDENCE JEFFERSON!

Pull yourself together! I've had QUITE enough trouble from you today! Now, what's this NONSENSE that Jinny's been telling me about the garden?" And Big Clara grabbed my arm, and marched me away from the scullery. She flung open the

garden door – and stopped dead as she saw the perfect rows of flowers.

"Strike me down with a rolling-pin!" she gasped.

I tried not to look too pleased with myself. "Yes," I said. "And now, if you please, I should find Prue, and—"

Big Clara turned, and stared at me, and a very uncomfortable little feeling crept into my stomach.

"I don't know what you're playing at, young lady," she said, "but I think you'd better stop it right now. I can see the flowers are sorted, and I'm pleased. And you've polished all that silver. And I'm a woman of her word, so you'll ALL be going to the Garden Party tomorrow...but we'll have no more nonsense about you looking for yourself, IF you please. Now, all three of you – into that kitchen!" And she turned and stalked back inside, leaving me staring after her.

"Moira," I said, and I could hear my voice wobbling, "Jinny – who do YOU think I am?"

"You're Princess Alice," Moira said. "Isn't she, Jinny?"

Jinny nodded. "Yes. But she DOES look a bit like Prue...and it's never a good idea to argue with Big Clara!"

I couldn't believe my ears. I swallowed hard...but then there was a MASSIVE roar, and Jinny and Moira seized my hands and whizzed me into the hot and steamy kitchen where Big Clara was waiting for us.

I'd never even DREAMT of a soup saucepan as big as the one bubbling away in the Princess Academy kitchen! Big Clara was stirring it with an ENORMOUS wooden spoon.

"Hurry along, girls!" she ordered. "Everything needs to be

out on those trays – we've got fifty hungry princesses waiting for their supper! Moira – you fetch the bowls! Jinny – fetch the spoons! Prue – cut up the bread!"

And there I was, slicing up a loaf of bread as if my life depended on it!

I'd cut up nearly the whole loaf when Big Clara came over to see how I was doing.

"Roll me up in a pancake!" she snorted. "Whatever's come over you, girl? You'll have to start all over again – Princesses like their bread thin and dainty!"

"No they don't!" I wailed, and I knew sounded TOTALLY pathetic – but I just couldn't help it. My feet hurt, my arms ached, and I'd cut my finger twice...and I was too tired to think of ANY way of escaping apart from just running for it...and then what would happen to the real Prue when she came back?

"Don't you go telling ME what princesses like!" Big Clara bellowed. "Now, you take this, and you slice it so thinly I can see the daylight shining through!" And she slapped another ENORMOUS loaf onto the board in front of me. "Or are you afraid of hard work all of a sudden? You never used to be!"

Did I burst into tears? Oh – SO nearly! But I didn't. If Prue wasn't afraid of hard work then neither was I.

I took a deep breath, and told myself I was a Perfect Princess, and I could do it!

I said, "Yes, Cook Clara," just as politely as I could, gritted my teeth – and started all over again...

...EXACTLY as there was a LOUD knock on the door. Jinny ran to open it, and there were my wonderful WONDERFUL best friends arm in arm, with Prue hiding behind them – and they were ALL smiling from ear to ear!!!!!!!!

Chapter Four

Have you ever tried to hug and be hugged by lots of people at once? It's very difficult, especially when there's a VERY large and muddled grown-up trying to work out what's going on. At last Big Clara gave one of her MAMMOTH bellows.

"Will somebody PLEASE tell me why my kitchen is FULL of princesses?" she demanded.

Princess Sophia stepped forward, and made one of her deepest curtsies.

"PLEASE forgive us, dear Cook Clara," she said, and she sounded

SO cool. "We came to thank you for all the truly delicious meals you have given us. We just LOVE your stews, and your fishcakes, and your pizza—"

She stopped, and looked blank for a second. Charlotte quickly chipped in.

"That's right!" she said – and nudged me hard. I looked round, and Prue was beckoning to me, her finger on her lips. And while Charlotte, Daisy, Katie and Emily explained to Big Clara how FABULOUS her cooking was, Prue and I sneaked into the scullery and swapped clothes.

"Thanks!" Prue whispered. "You're a STAR!"

"Wherever did you go?" I asked. "I thought I was going to be here for EVER! And I'm USELESS at cutting bread!"

Prue's eyes twinkled. "After I'd polished the silver I peeped out to see what you were doing," she said, "but you were still busy. So I went to look at that famous staircase of yours...and Queen Mum Mattie was making a DREADFUL fuss because you hadn't come back!"

"Oh dear," I said, and my heart sank. "I'll be in HUGE trouble now..."

"Queen Mother Matilda saw me, and thought I was you," Prue went on, "and she said she HOPED I wouldn't fall down the stairs THIS time...and Princess Daisy whispered to me that you were the only one left who hadn't passed her test!"

I was beginning to feel positively sick. "Oh NO," I moaned. "I'll be the ONLY PERSON who can't go to the Garden Party tomorrow!"

Prue shook her head, and

twinkled even more. "You'll be there, Princess Alice!" she said. "You were so kind, and you sorted out the flower vase for me – so I floated down the staircase for you. And guess what? Queen Mum Mattie gave me TEN tiara points!"

"That's right!" Charlotte was standing in the scullery doorway, grinning at us. "Prue was FANTASTIC!"

"WOW!" I could hardly believe it. Prue had passed my test for me, AND got me ten tiara points...but a voice was buzzing in my head. *Isn't that cheating?*

And I suddenly felt REALLY uncomfortable, because Prue was looking SO pleased because she thought she'd helped me.

"Thank you VERY much," I said, and I tried to sound as if I meant it.

Prue giggled. "No worries. I'm just SO glad I'm not a princess! It was fun for today, but I'd HATE to have to do that sort of thing all the time!" And then she gave me a little wave, and skipped off into the kitchen just as the bell rang for six o'clock supper.

I limped back to the dining hall with Sophia and the others.

My feet were sore, but I didn't mind. It looked as if I was going to go to the Garden Party after all...AND I was going to see the Magical Mirror. I just couldn't quite stop that little voice, though. *Perfect Princesses never EVER cheat* it whispered, over and over again.

Chapter Five

Perfect Princesses never EVER cheat!

I could hardly sleep that night. And when we woke up, and dressed in our best dresses, I could hardly breathe. Charlotte said it was excitement, but I knew it was something quite different. I was TOTALLY quaking inside, because I knew what I HAD to do if I was ever going to be a Perfect Princess.

My dress was GORGEOUS! It rustled beautifully as I slipped it over my head, and when I danced round the skirts swirled and swished. We took turns in helping each other with our hair and our tiaras, and then it was time to go across to Fairy G's study...and we were just in time to see Princess Perfecta and Princess Floreen coming out.

"I'm SURE I deserve more tiara points than YOU," Perfecta was saying angrily.

"I've only got ONE more than you," Floreen said. "I only had—"

Perfecta suddenly noticed us

listening, and she absolutely
GLARED.

"SHHH!" she snapped at
Floreen, and they scuttled away
as fast as they could go.

We were all feeling REALLY nervous as we knocked on Fairy G's door.

Especially me...

...and then the door opened, and Fairy G called, "COME IN!"

Fairy G looked WONDERFUL. She doesn't usually dress up, but she was wearing an AMAZING flowery dress covered in sparkly gold roses, and a long green velvet cloak embroidered with silver butterflies...and their wings were actually fluttering! You could tell at once that she was a really IMPORTANT Fairy Godmother.

We couldn't help curtseying, and she laughed her big booming laugh.

"Now, Rose Room – do you want to be presented to the mirror one by one, or all together?"

Of course we wanted to be together!

Fairy G laughed again, and waved her wand...and all of a sudden the shelves full of pots and herbs and potions vanished.

Instead we could see an ENORMOUS mirror, with a strange twisted dark wood frame...and we could see our reflections, standing in a row, and holding hands.

"Are you ready?" Fairy G asked.

I gulped.

"If you please, Fairy G," I said, and my voice sounded very wobbly. "I have something important to say."

I stepped forward, and I could feel my friends staring at me in surprise. "You see, I've got ten tiara points that aren't really mine. And I failed *Descending the Staircase as if Walking on Air*...so I shouldn't be here at all. And I'm VERY sorry..." I had to stop to rub my eyes, "...that I didn't say anything before, but I did SO want to wear my dress – even if it was only for the morning...and now I'll go back to Rose Room, and—"

"STOP!"

I couldn't believe it. Fairy G was actually SMILING at me!!!! "I think, Princess Alice," she said, "we should let the Magical Mirror decide, don't you?" And she waved her wand, and there was an EXPLOSION of a million zillion little sparkles of twinkling light.

And as we stared in total amazement a truly BEAUTIFUL voice spoke to us from the very depths of the mirror.

"Well done, Princess Alice," it said. "You have been honest, and that is an excellent quality in a princess. You must remember that no Princess is so Perfect that she never ever makes a mistake..." The voice paused, and gave a funny little chuckle. "Besides, the Rose Room Princesses make me laugh..." and for a SECOND there was a flash of a picture in the mirror – and it was me rolling down the stairs, and my friends staring with big round eyes, and Queen Mum Mattie looking HORRIFIED!!

Fairy G gave a little cough.

"Sorry, Fairy G," the mirror said, "but it WAS funny! Now, where was I? Oh yes. Ahem. I have MUCH pleasure in awarding the Princesses Alice, Katie, Emily, Charlotte, Daisy and Sophia three hundred tiara points to share between them...

...and you may ALL go to the Garden Party!"

Chapter Six

What was the Garden Party like? Oh, it was FABULOUS!!! And would you believe that I actually DID float down the Grand Staircase? I think it must have been because I was so happy! And the flowers in the gardens were GLORIOUS...and we danced and danced and danced to the music of the orchestra. My Grandfather was so pleased the mirror had given me fifty tiara points he nearly twirled me into a lemonade fountain...but my Grandmother caught us just in time.

Late that night, when we were lying in our beds in Rose Room, I tried yet again to make the others take more tiara points than me...but they wouldn't.

"All for one, and one for all," Sophia said sleepily. "And we're ALL going to win enough points to be members of the Tiara Club, and have a lovely lovely LOVELY time..."

And I smiled, and blew her a kiss...

...and one to you too.

What happens next?
Find out in

Princess Sophia
and the Sparkling Surprise

Hello! My name is Princess Sophia, and I'm SO pleased you're keeping us company here at the Princess Academy. Have you met the others from Rose Room? There's Alice, and Katie, and Daisy and Charlotte and Emily, and we've been best friends ever since we met on the very first day of term. We all look after each other. Which is a Very Good Thing when there are princesses like Perfecta around. She's so MEAN! Alice's big sister says Perfecta got hardly ANY tiara points in her first year at the Academy, and Queen Gloriana (that's our head teacher) wouldn't let her join the fabulous Tiara Club. She had to repeat a year, so she's here with us, and that means TROUBLE!

Check out

The
Tiara
Club

website at:

www.tiaraclub.co.uk

You'll find Perfect Princess games and fun
things to do, as well as news on the Tiara
Club and all your favourite princesses!